Beneath the Mask

Vulnerable Villainess, Volume 0

Nikki Larousse

Published by N.L. Ink Publishing, 2022.

This is a work of fiction. Similarities to real people, places, or events are entirely coincidental.

BENEATH THE MASK

First edition. January 25, 2022.

ISBN: 979-8230640554

Written by Nikki Larousse.

Table of Contents

For those who wanted to have a *happily ever after with their enemy* but were afraid to do so in real life.

This one is for *you*.

Prologue

I, Ashley Banner, was sitting by *myself* on a Friday night in a downtown bar. I was looking at my drink. I sighed before I sipped on my apple martini before someone took a seat beside me.

I did not know who it was, but it smelled of aftershave, *pine* and *mint*. I knew it was a male. I smirked inwardly.

I was tossing my hair on one side of my shoulder, trying to be sexy, when I didn't even know if the male was looking at me.

"One whiskey on ice, please,"

His baritone voice was making shudders down my spine. I tried so hard not to show that I was interested in the male beside me. The bartender nodded at the male before he poured one into the glass, handing it to him.

I waited as I was wishing him to go away. *Secretly*, I was hoping that he would stay. I don't know what to think but to sip on my martini.

Then, *that* baritone voice was heard again.

"What a rough night," he said, not knowing that he might be talking to me. I turned slowly to see the male that was assumed to be talking to me. And I sucked my breath when I was taking him in, capturing his features into my brain for the rest of my life.

His hazel eyes were burning into my emerald orbs as I was looking at his black hair. It was shining like moonlight was glistening in them. I thought it was just the dim lighting in this bar. I smiled.

"And what makes it a *rough* night, sir?" I asked, sipping again on my martini. His gaze was locking on my lips as I was smacking them, making sure that my tongue was sticking out. I was licking my lower lips. He smirked.

"*Someone* was making me have difficulty saying a proper sentence tonight," he said as he was sipping on his whiskey, making sure that I was looking at his twinkling hazel eyes.

I chuckled, playing with the rim of my glass.

"Oh?"

"And I was wondering if she was *occupied* tonight, perhaps waiting for *someone*?" he said smoothly.

I was smiling seductively at him, batting my eyelashes.

"And what will *you* do if she doesn't?" I asked, noting that he was playing a game with me.

The male chuckled before he put his glass down and turned his lean, muscular body toward me. He extended his hand for me to shake as he introduced himself.

"Ashton Flammen, nice to meet you, Miss..."

"Ashley Banner. It's a pleasure," I said as I took his rough, calloused hand.

Electric was running through my spine at the contact. I was smiling at him, taking in every feature that was on his face. Then, we dropped our hands.

"Flammen, you say? Is that some kind of another language?" I said, as I knew it was not a common surname.

Ashton chuckled lowly, leaning closer to my ear. I angled my body so that he could see the top of my cleavage.

"It's German for flames. My father thought it would be fun to have a surname in honour of Rhein in Flammen," Ashton said. I chuckled at his joke.

"He had a very dry sense of humour then," I said, taking my apple martini again as I was looking at the hazel eyes. Ashton smirked.

"So, if you're not too busy, shall we go somewhere *else*?" he asked.

I was arching my eyebrow. The man laughed.

"I was hoping that I could get to know you better," he said before settling his empty glass down.

I put my martini down and glanced at the watch. It was almost ten in the evening. I shrugged.

"Why not?" I said, reaching for my purse to pay for my drink. Ashton stopped me.

"Please, allow me," he said. I shook my head, declining his generous offer.

"We're not on a date, and I can certainly pay for my drinks," I said as I put a twenty-note down.

Ashton laughed as he was allowing me to go first. I got off my stool. I noticed his eyes were travelling down my long legs as I was wearing a short black dress with a matching stiletto.

I *knew* what it did to my legs.

I walked ahead of him, leaving the bar. I felt the body heat behind me. Ashton was tall, a few inches taller than me, as we walked side by side. I kept my hands to my sides.

Suddenly, Ashton was dumping his coat onto my shoulders. I looked at him. He smiled.

"It looks like you're freezing. I don't want to kill you since it was my invitation to get out of that bar," Ashton said. I laughed. He smiled.

"I never thought you would be a considerate person, Ashton," I said, tasting my tongue on his given name.

I liked it—no scratch that—I *loved* it.

"Your laughter is nice. I never made a woman laugh before," he replied.

We were looking out on the pier. I looked at Ashton as he was staring out into the horizon where the boats and yachts were settling in. I smiled.

"Then they don't have a sense of humour," I said. Ashton looked at me.

"I guess they don't then," he said, stepping closer to me. I was looking up at his face when he was reaching out to caress my cheek. I let him.

"I never encountered someone like you before, Ashley Banner," he said huskily as he was staring into my eyes. His hazel eyes were twinkling. I smiled.

"Then, I don't think you want me to go then," I said as I was moving closer to him, gripping his shirt as I was licking my lower lips.

His gaze was focused on them. Then, he shook his head, wanting to withdraw. I did not give him a chance since I was pulling him closer and kissing his lips.

The first thought that came to my mind *was soft*. Soft and smooth as I was kissing Ashton. I don't think that Ashton would kiss a woman as he did to me right now, for I know when a guy looked at me with *lust* in his eyes...

Perhaps I cannot simply compare him to *anyone* after all.

I moved my lips against him, and Ashton moved in sync. I moaned, moving my hands to grip his neck. I was arching my back, grazing my nipples against him. Right after that, Ashton broke the kiss.

"We *shouldn't*," he said as I was arching my eyebrow, still clinging myself to him.

"Shouldn't *what*?"

Ashton shook his head. He was about to turn away. But I stopped him.

I stopped him because all I wanted was to forget who I was in one night. In *his* arms.

"Just for tonight?" I asked him as his hazel eyes were looking at me. I smiled, pulling him away from the pier as I only had one destination in mind.

Bed and that will be *my* bed in *my* home.

WE HARDLY PASSED THE front door as Ashton was kissing me again. He pushed me into the household, hitting my back against the door. I don't know if it was his nature to be *rough* and *hard*.

I *loved* it.

I was kissing him fervently as he was finding the zipper of my dress in the back. He unzipped it as my hands were tearing his shirt. I sent the buttons flying on the floor. He chuckled.

"*Feisty*," Ashton whispered huskily when I was gripping his neck and kissed him again.

"Talk later," I said, pushing him toward the bed that was located at the end of the studio. I was straddling him as Ashton was sitting at the edge. He was roaming my sides with his rough hands. I fumbled with his belt. He chuckled.

"Slow down, kitten," he said before he flipped me over.

I was on my back on the mattress. I was breathing hard as I was left in my panties. My nipples were hardened. I looked at Ashton's darkened hazel eyes that were taking in my half-nakedness.

"You're *beautiful*, Ashley," he said as he kneeled in front of me when a ripping sound was heard.

I looked at him in shock. Ashton was smirking at me.

"Now, for the dessert," he said as he was spreading my thighs. I have been wet ever since I smelled his aftershave.

When his eyes were on me, I bit my lower lips as I could sense my nectar was flowing down my core.

"*Guten appetit*," Ashton said before dove between my thighs.

I arched my back. I was gripping Ashton's hair while his tongue did wicked things to me. I was breathing hard, looking at the ceiling.

That was when I felt his finger *inside* me.

"*Fuck*, you're tight," Ashton hissed. I moaned. His delectable mouth was *feasting* on my clit. I was sucking in deep breaths as he was sucking and licking it as if he owned it.

A wave of pleasure came over me. I arched my back as Ashton's hands were fondling my breasts. He chuckled.

Then, Ashton was positioning himself between me. There was a question inside his eyes as his tip was at my entrance. I nodded at him as he moved forward, plunging me with his cock inside my core.

Then, I shouted his name, for all I knew was only *pleasure* in his arms after that night.

Chapter 1

Well, *that* was the first night I had known my significant other, Ashton, on one Friday evening. He spent the night with me, and he even made breakfast after that. He kissed me goodbye and asked me to go on a date next weekend. I said *yes*, and everything has been history.

We have been going steady for about a month as a couple. Ashton told me that he worked as a civil servant at a government office, and I told him that I was an IT engineer at a company. We went on picnics sometimes, and today was one of *those* days.

"Ash, hurry up. We're going to be late, and I don't want to be inside when the sun is out," I shouted from the stairs. I have moved from the pier to buy a house. Ashton had moved in with me ever since.

"You know, Ashley, you're being *restless*. It was supposed to be *our* day together," Ashton said, chuckling at my enthusiasm.

I was rolling my eyes, taking the picnic basket as I was heading out to the car.

"Can you at least get the door?" I said. My boyfriend kissed me.

"Sure, *liebling*," Ashton said before I smiled. I walked out of the house, and he went to get the locks in.

I put the basket inside the trunk before I closed it. Ashton went to the driver's side, and I took the passenger seat. I fastened my seatbelt as Ashton ignited the engine and drove off from our driveway.

"So, where are we going today?" he asked me as he put his hand on my knee, rolling his thumb in small circles.

I was looking out of the window at the scenery. I turned my face around, staring at Ashton. I put my hand on top of his over my knee.

"Hmm, what about the beach? I heard that it's a good day for *swimming*," I suggested.

Ashton smirked. His eyes were concealed behind the sunglasses he wore. My straight, brunette hair was whipping against the wind as we were rolling down the street to our favourite, secluded spot at the public beach.

Ashton stopped the car and switched off the engine. I got out of my seat and stared at the horizon of the beach.

"So beautiful," I said breathlessly when Ashton was standing next to me.

"But not as beautiful as *you*," he whispered huskily, hugging me from behind.

I chuckled as I leaned closer to him. He kissed my neck before I got the basket, and we headed on to the beach.

I opened the basket after Ashton set up the mat. I laid out the food. There's roasted chicken and bread. I pulled out some fruits and looked at the beach. There was no one in this area. I was breathing happily as I was tying my hair in a ponytail.

"This is *delicious*," Ash said with his mouth full. I was smiling at him. The wind dishevelled his hair as I was taking in his features. He was so handsome and beautiful, like Apollo, the Greek god of poetry and music. I don't think I would be lucky enough to have him as my boyfriend.

Feeling my stare on his face, Ashton wiped his mouth. He was looking at me, arching his eyebrow in question.

"What?" he asked before I shook my head.

"Nothing,"

"It's always mean *something* if you say nothing, Ashley. I know you have something on your mind, so spit it out, or I will have to get it out of you," he teased, his eyes sparkling with amusement, and I couldn't help but giggle in response.

It was as if he could read my mind, my every thought and feeling. No one, I meant *no one*, understood me as he did.

"Well, I was thinking that it might be a good time for me to go swimming. *Alone*," I said as I stood up. I took off my dress. I wore a bikini underneath it when I felt Ashton was staring at me. I smiled at him as his darkened gaze travelled down my body. Then, I was off to the shore.

The water was clear blue, and the beach was clean. I was waddling into the waves. Then, I was diving underneath it.

The water was warm enough as I was swimming around the shore, which was located near the alcove. I swam to the surface, breaking the water surface, and took a deep breath.

I looked at where Ashton was sitting, but it was empty. I turned around to see where he was until *someone* was coming from *behind* me.

I shrieked in shock. Ashton was laughing at me. He pulled me into his arms, kissing me on the lips. I wound my hands into his wet hair as the sun was making his eyes look like gold.

"I love you, you know *that*, right?" he asked, his eyes filled with the depth of his feelings. I couldn't help but roll my eyes at his silly question, knowing that his love for me was as constant as the sun rising each day.

"You tell me every single day, Ash. Of course, I *know*, and I love you too," I said and meant.

Ashton smiled before he moved us toward the alcove. We had never swum there before, but as soon as we were inside, Ashton was bringing us closer to the edge. Then, we climbed over.

I looked around, taking in the scenery in front of me. The sunlight reflected on the water. It gave off lights inside the alcove. I don't think I have seen anything like this before. I was about to ask Ashton before I saw something *unexpected*.

Ashton was on one knee, holding out his hand as he was gripping a ring. I realized an engagement ring with topaz at the centre and tiny diamonds around it.

My hands flew to my mouth as I was choking on the upcoming sob in my mouth.

Ashton cleared his throat, looking at me with all the love that shone inside his eyes.

"Ashley Banner, I know that we only knew for a month, but my heart was saying that I wish to know you for the rest of my life. I know I will never be good enough, but will you at least give me a chance to honour me by being my wife?" he asked me as I was sobbing now.

He smiled when I dropped to my knees in front of him. I was hugging him but could not form any reply, for I was sobbing right now.

"Is *this* a yes?" he asked me, chuckling softly. I nodded, burying my face inside his neck. Hugging him, smelling him, loving him. It was all the things that kept me together, and I know that he will do that honour for the rest of my life.

"I love you, Ashley Banner, and I will always be," he said as I was sobbing even more when he put his ring on me.

I was kissing him, and he claimed my mouth, tears and all. I landed on my back in the dirt.

Ashton was roaming his hands on my body. My nipples were hard. I was arching my back as he was kissing my neck. Then, he went to my nipples.

"Now, I think we can celebrate it," Ashton said huskily, removing my bikini and his swim trunks. He showed me how much he loved me in that alcove over and over again until our hands were pruned from it.

"I CANNOT BELIEVE IT. You're *engaged*," my friend—Aleena—told me as I was looking at the food that would be served for our engagement party. I smiled when Aleena was putting the drinks on the other side of the table.

"I know. I was so happy that I did not dare to think that it was a dream," I said. Aleena giggled at me. Then, she was staring at Ashton, who was talking to Hermon, our childhood friend.

Aleena's *lifelong* crush.

"So, will you ever make a move on *him*?" I asked her quietly. Aleena sighed. She rubbed her neck, smiling at me.

"I don't know. It was hard to think that Ashton would ever consider *me* as someone worthy of being his *girlfriend*. Let alone his *wife*," she said as I was looking at him.

Hermon laughed at something Ashton said, and I smiled.

"It's a shame. Hermon is *very* good-looking," I said. Aleena scoffed and said something that I didn't quite catch.

"Sorry, *what*?" I asked her. She shook her head, and we walked around to greet the guests. Most of them were colleagues from my workplace, and some were from my hometown.

I moved back to my small hometown, where I mostly did my work online, but they never thought that I would be spending some time here again.

Since I was *keen* on leaving here, I was, again, back in my *backyard*.

"Ashley, it's time," Ashton said as I was excusing myself.

Aleena was nodding at me. I was walking up to the centre and gripping his arm. Ashton was kissing my cheek before someone was howling at us.

"Well, settle down, everyone." Ashton started, looking at all the attendees at our party. I was smiling up at him as he was looking around.

"I never thought that I could be happy in my life. Serving the government, making my own money, and living a comfortable life." Ashton said, looking over at me. I smiled as he smiled.

"But then, one night. I thought to myself if I was to be happy, I might as well share it with someone *else*. Then, here I was, stumbling at the bar, and I saw this *beautiful, magnificent* person sitting there alone on Friday night," he said.

I blushed, thinking of the memory that was just one month ago.

"I said to myself, '*Ashton, if you don't say hi, you might as well die*,'" he said. Some of the crowd laughed.

I smiled as I was squeezing my hands on him. He chuckled before his hazel eyes were looking at me.

"And the more I talked to that person on Friday night, the more alive I was after being alone for so long that I have found my light in my darkness. And you, my lovely Ashley, are my light till the end of our time together," Ashton said. He pulled me in and kissed me on the mouth.

I gripped his nape, and everything dawned upon us as the crowd cheered for the happy life that we would lead together.

If only I could see the *signs*.

Chapter 2

"Are you afraid?" Aleena asked me as I was taking a deep breath. I don't know if I was afraid on *my* wedding day. Everyone would have cold feet, but I don't think that was the issue right here.

I was happy and too overwhelmed that I would be marrying the person that I loved the most in the world.

No, I was not *afraid*.

"No, I don't think it was the wedding jitters. I think..." I bit my lower lips for the dramatic effect.

"I was looking forward to our lives together," I said as I was holding the bouquet that I got for my wedding. I was breathing hard before I turned to look at the altar.

Ashton was smiling as the bishop stood on the stage, and the wedding march was heard. The crowd stood, and I walked in as Aleena was in front of me as my maid of honour.

Here it goes.

I walked down the aisle as I was smiling at the crowd. For the twenty-four years that I have been alone, I never thought that I would find *someone* who loved me for who I was, for I have become.

I looked at Ashton as if he were immaculate in his black Armani suit before me. I was wearing an ivory A-line dress, and I was smiling from ear to ear.

Of course, a bride that shone on her wedding day.

I stood in front of Ashton as the music died. The bishop was attending to the crowd, ready to start the holy matrimony that I would never wish to escape ever.

"Dearly beloved, we gather here today to unite this man and this woman together as in a holy matrimony that they will be shared for the rest of their lives together." The bishop spoke as Ashton was leaning toward me.

"You look *beautiful*, liebling," he said as I was blushing.

I don't think that anyone would know I was a virgin, for I already gave it to Ashton when we were sleeping together after that night in the bar. I doubted that was the reason he married me right here.

Perhaps a *little* bit of it.

"And you look nice as well," I said, smiling while the bishop explained the importance of being together, not committing to infidelity and all that sort. I know Ashton would never seek out an *external* relationship if I satisfied him every night.

And I know *I* do a pretty good job at it.

"Do you, Ashton Flammen, take this woman as your lawful wife, in sickness and in health, in rich and poor, to cherish her love for as long as you both shall live?" he asked Ashton before my fiancé looked at me. He was smiling.

"I do,"

"And do you, Ashley Banner, take this man as your lawfully wedded husband, in sickness and in health, in rich and poor, to cherish his love for you as long as you both shall live?"

I looked at Ashton. His hazel eyes glistened like the first night we met. The black hair that I had known to touch and grip whenever we made love. I sucked a breath and breathed out the word that I had longed to say.

"I do,"

"And by the power that was rested on me, I pronounce you husband and wife. You may kiss your bride," the bishop said, blessing the union.

Ashton pulled me in by the nape and kissed me like the first time we met.

Passionate, *wild*, and *free*.

The crowd cheered before I could focus on them because Ashton Flammen had been mine forever, and I was his until death tore us apart.

"IT'S A VERY GRAND RECEPTION," Aleena told me as I was sipping on the champagne as we were celebrating my wedding reception.

It was late afternoon, and we continued the party till evening. It was *exhilarating* and *nervous*, as I would be spending time in Ashton's bed a couple of hours later.

As his *wife*, he is no longer his girlfriend or fiancée. I can *hardly* wait.

"Well," I said as I was jerking my head toward Hermon before Aleena was looking at him.

"I can see that he was having the best time in his life, that bloody wanker," I chuckled. I noticed that Aleena was gripping her glass.

Hermon was dancing on the dance floor and was attracting quite several admirers, mostly *women*.

Aleena scoffed as she drank her wine. "He certainly does love the attention," she said before I smiled.

Then, I noticed that Ashton was making his way toward me.

"I need to go. My husband is coming," I said wickedly. Aleena made a vulgar gesture at me. I laughed.

"I think you should find yourself a boyfriend, Aleena, and perhaps *he* will notice you then,"

It was harsh advice, but when your best friends simply do not confess their love for each other, I might as well jump in between them.

"Ready for our dance, liebling?" Ashton asked me. I was nodding at him. He pulled me toward the dance floor before the music was playing.

La Cumpusita, the tango music.

The musicians were playing the chords. My husband was smirking at me. I narrowed my eyes at him as I knew that he was trying to test my dancing shoes.

Well, I *show* him.

He moved like a panther across the dance floor. I was returning the gesture. I swayed my hips as I smirked seductively at him.

Ashton was surprised, but he did not seem to mind that I had something else up my sleeves.

We were joining together at the centre as I was dropping my hands in his. Ashton turned me around as his chest was hitting my bareback against my wedding dress.

"I don't know you tango, liebling," he whispered inside my ear.

I slid to the floor, and he still held my hands as I slid across the floor, showing him my flexibility. Then, I was standing in front of him again with my calf upon his leg.

"Well then, you don't know about my *flexibility* as well. I thought you already knew that," I teased Ashton as I was arching my eyebrow at him.

Ashton chuckled when he was bending me backwards. He was kissing my throat. I shivered.

"Then, I would love to know more about it," he whispered before I was turning in his arms again. We swayed to the music as Ashton led me.

I smiled at him, batting my eyelashes before he spun me out of his arm and called me back in. I hit his hard chest again as his hand was on my waist.

I gasped as I could sense the erection on my backbone. I glanced at Ashton over my shoulder.

"You're *incorrigible,*"

"And you *love* me anyway," he whispered huskily as we swayed together.

We were at the final stage of dancing. I swayed my hips against Ashton, noting that he growled in my ears.

Then, Ashton dipped me back, and I was arching my legs around his calves. The music stopped. Everybody cheered as Ashton slid me up against his hard body.

I did not miss a muscle underneath his suit.

I was breathless, and when I looked at his darkened hazel eyes, I knew he wanted to escape.

"Shall we get going?" I asked him as I was smirking. He growled even more.

"Absolutely,"

ASHTON PUSHED ME ACROSS the suite as he was kissing me, claiming my mouth. His hands were busy trying to find the zipper of my wedding gown. He dragged it down. He was shoving it off my shoulders, leaving me with only my undergarment.

I shoved his coat off his shoulders, ripping his buttons off. Ashton chuckled lowly when I was fumbling with his belt.

He pushed me backwards as my legs hit the bed. I landed on the mattress. My breasts were bouncing up and down.

"So energetic, but I want to be in control tonight," Ashton said as he looked down at me.

I growled before I was on my knees. I was looking at the visible tent in front of Ashton's pants. I smirked as I was tracing my fingers on it.

"Do you want to? Or should I be down on my knees and pleasure you with my mouth?" I said as I was licking my lips. His eyes darkened even more before he grunted.

"Do it,"

I was crawling on my knees as I was locking my eyes with my husband. I pulled his belt before I unbuttoned the pants. I dragged it down his hips with his briefs. I looked at his eager length. I smirked.

"Not so in control, are you now?"

"Suck it. Suck it with your *mouth*," Ashton growled huskily. I was putting my hands on his thighs. His very *muscular* thighs.

I was looking at the red part of the head of his cock, oozing with pre-cum. I was licking the underside. Ash groaned as I was gripping the base of his cock.

"*Yes*," he moaned, gripping my hair. I was putting his tip inside me, tasting him with my tongue as Ashton gasped.

"Ashley," he said before I was sucking him whole. He hissed at the sensation, and I was happy to oblige him. I moaned, bobbing my head up and down.

"Oh, yes. *Yes*!" Ashton said as I was playing with his balls and gripped him at the base. Ashton threw his head back before I could sense that he was going to come.

My core was wet from this foreplay when Ashton was pulling me by the hair, and I was pushed against the mattress.

"No more. I want to be inside you. *Now*!" Ashton grunted. He was spreading my thighs in front of him, and with one swift move, he was inside me.

I gasped as Ash groaned on top of me. He moved in and out of me, building the pleasure inside me.

I was arching my back as he was sucking on my tips and playing with my clit. Then, I was at my peak and came down from it with his name on my lips.

"*Ashton*,"

My walls clenched his cock. Ashton was shaking on top of me, spewing his hot seed into my womb. I kissed his mouth. We were playing with our tongues before he nuzzled my neck.

"Mine, you're mine, Ashley. *Mine*," he said as he kissed me. Then, he sucked on my throat, leaving me a hickey that I would be proud to wear and showed it to the world.

And you're mind, Ashton Flammen, nobody can take you away from me now, I mused thoughtfully as I played with his hair.

A promise that seemed *harmless* at the time, but then, what do we know of our future, right?

Chapter 3

It has been a year since our wedding. We went to Italy for our honeymoon, and surprisingly, Ashton could speak fluently, whereas I was trying to capture what he was saying at the moment.

I have no gift for languages, for I was more into mechanical stuff like machines.

Perhaps that was why we completed each other so well.

The routine was simple. We woke together, showered, and then had breakfast before we went to the workplace.

On the weekend, it was slightly different for Ashton, who would be making love to me on Friday night, not letting me have a wink of sleep.

Then, we made love again in the morning, and I was happy to oblige with his morning wood. Afterwards, we had dessert in the shower before we went to have some breakfast, naked, as Ashton would feed me food while I was on his lap.

Such life was for a *normal* couple. And we were normal until that one day when he had to leave for an outstation work.

"Honey, hurry up! Or you will be late for work," I shouted from downstairs, making my husband rush in everything he was doing at the moment.

"Coming," Ashton shouted from our bedroom while taking his briefcase and trying to make sure his tie was neat.

I was looking from the kitchen as he was running down the stairs. I shook my head at his rush before I offered to help him.

"Here. Let me help you," I offered to make Ashton's tie.

My fingers expertly did the tie while he was checking me out, his *wife*. I stood there in the black dress that Ashton had brought for my birthday, which fell to my knees, and a black stiletto. I noticed that he was staring before I arched my eyebrow.

"Do you have something in mind that you want to share, Mr. Flammen?" I asked as I was fixing his tie.

My husband smirked before his hands were on my waist, pulling me closer as my breasts were touching his hard chest.

Desire flew inside me, but I kept my face as stoic as I could.

"And what will *you* do if I have such thoughts?" Ashton asked me as I was looking into his hazel eyes. He was smirking at me. I was rolling my eyes, and a smile was on my lips.

"Well, perhaps I will be obliged to entertain you since it will be the last time for me to see you before your two weeks outstation," I said as Ashton was leaning in.

"I was thinking that perhaps I wanted to taste your tasty lips. What will you do?" Ashton asked me huskily with that baritone voice of his, making me jumpy altogether.

My core was *instantly* wet. I think I have to change my panties before I turn in for work as well.

"You're *insatiable*," I said, pulling his tie, and we're kissing now. His hands were roaming on my hips before he was gripping my buttocks firmly.

I gasped when he slid his tongue inside me, tasting like fresh mint. I was moulding my lithe body to his.

Ashton broke the kiss before he breathed out, smiling wickedly with his full, kissable lips.

"You will be the *death* of me," he said huskily. I was turning away from him, making sure that my brunette, straight hair flowed smoothly on my back and ended on my waist as I was walking to the kitchen.

I smirked before I put the omelette and sausages on the table. Ashton was sitting at the counter, looking at my swollen lips. My lustrous lips, red lipstick that he had ruined now.

"Eat now. I don't want you to be on an empty stomach when you're on your flight. What would people think if my husband's stomach was growling inside the aeroplane?" I said, taking one of the sausages and sucking on them. Ashton's eyes were on mine as I was smirking while I bit on it.

"I will be busy when I get there. I don't think I will have some time to chat with you while abroad," Ash said, digging into the breakfast. I nodded at him as I was sipping on the orange juice.

"Me too. The boss wanted something that I don't think everyone was willing to take on the project, so he dumped on me," I said as I was rolling my eyes. I sighed loudly.

Suddenly, Ashton was asking me to come to his side. I went, and he pulled me on his lap.

"You think you can be late for once?" he asked me as I was straddling his lap. His erection was noticeable. I smirked.

"What do you have in mind?" I purred at him as I was gripping his tie. The tie that I just made for him as he was rushing to get them right.

"*Hmm*, I don't know, but a quickie would make my mood much better for our two-week separation," he said as I pulled my dress up to my waist.

Ashton was fumbling with his belt. His cock sprang free, and I was positioned to be at my entrance. I was *wet* ever since I was making his tie before he slammed into me.

I moaned, gripping his tie and his nape. He pushed me up and down his length as I was breathing hard.

"Now, this is the way to say goodbye," I said as I bit his lower lips. Ashton growled before he slammed me onto the counter and pushed the plates aside.

"And *you* are the most delicious meal ever," my husband said as I was arching my back.

The sensation was near, and with two more strokes, I came as Ashton spewed his hot semen with our names on each other lips.

After that, he kissed me again in a passionate, demanding way before he went out and drove away from our driveway.

I was sighing as I was washing the dishes. I picked up my briefcase after I fixed my dress and hair. I can't just go to the workplace like my husband has ravished me.

My engagement ring shone as I was getting out of the house, smiling the whole way to my workplace.

I WAS LOOKING AT THE skyscraper where I was working right now. After I left our house, I went to the workplace, looking like a woman so much in love with her husband.

And I was the luckiest woman in the world for being able to get married to such a wonderful man like Ashton. I giggled before I swiped my card and I was walking inside the building.

"What's got you into a good mood this morning?" Aleena asked me before I looked at her. She was glowing as well, and perhaps her makeup was flawless today. I blinked.

"And why are you wearing makeup? Got any hot dates tonight?" I asked curiously. Aleena smirked.

"What would *you* like to know?" she replied before I rolled my eyes. We were in front of the elevator, and Aleena punched the buttons.

"Well, if you must know, even though we will be missing each other for two weeks, Ash just gave me the best farewell gift ever. I was so happy because it would remind me of him until he came back," I said, stepping into the elevator.

No one dared to follow us, for this elevator was only for our workplace.

Aleena arched her eyebrow at me. "Really, and what is that gift?" she asked before I was smirking at her.

"Can't you guess?"

"*Gross*, but I am happy for you. Have you been talking to Ashton about your dream lately?" she asked me.

I was biting my lower lips. I shrugged, not wanting to discuss anything further, for Aleena knew that she could not push me.

Not until I asked Ashton if he wanted to start our family yet.

I sighed as the elevator dinged and our assistants greeted us. I took off my coat and briefcase before I handed them to my assistant. She informed me that my boss, Megan, wanted to speak with me about a certain project.

"I catch you later," I said as I sipped on the coffee. Aleena was making it to her cubicle. Saying that I was an IT engineer was a lie, for I never thought that I would have to lie to my husband.

No, that was only a front for me to cover who I was.

An *assassin*. A *hired hitman*. A *markswoman*.

I sighed when my stiletto clicked on the marble floor as I made my way to Megan's office. She was the director of the secret service that we served the government. We were supposed to be a mystery, but lately, Megan has been itchy about something.

Something that she will be telling me now.

I knocked on the door and heard someone calling from inside.

"Come in," Megan said before I opened the door. She was typing away on her keyboard, not so much to be looking at me.

"So, what is it that you want to talk to me this morning?" I asked as I was sitting in front of her desk. Megan was typing away before she sipped on her coffee. Then, she was turning her gaze upon me.

Her blue-grey eyes were locking on my dress. *Assessing* me. *Calculating*. *Deadly*. Then, she smiled.

"I see that you glow today. How's married life treating you?" she asked before I shrugged.

"Same old, same old. Well, the sex was getting better, however," I said.

Megan made a face at me. Then, she cleared her throat.

"Anyway, I have a new mission," she said as I turned my head to look at her.

"And his name is Frederic Rhein."

Chapter 4

"He's a spy who was led into our country to learn more about our military defences before he can contact his informant. We caught him leaving last night after thorough research in the cameras and the matching profiles that we can get our hands on," Megan explained. She snatched something from the table and read it out loud.

"His destination is unknown for all that matters because someone on his side has deleted everything before we can get it. It was a miracle that we were still able to track him after that," Megan said as she put the paper down.

I looked at it as I was grazing every detail that I could get on it.

"When do I leave?" I asked her as Megan was smirking at me.

"Immediately,"

I WAS HEAVING AND VOMITING into the bowl of the toilet as I was gripping the edge of it. I breathed hard as I looked at the contents of my empty stomach. I just got out of Megan's office when something caught my nose, and I rushed to the toilet.

Ginger, it has to be *ginger*.

I sighed before I pulled the flusher, and the water was cleaning my mess. I was breathing hard. Then, I pulled myself up as I was rearranging my dress and my stiletto.

Well, it will be a long time before I can wear one again.

I gripped my stomach as Aleena's warning was coming into my head. I haven't told Ashton yet what I was keeping from him. It has been 2 weeks, and the signs were already showing.

How I wanted him so bad now and then. The taste of the food was different, and I was eating more than I supposed. Ginger was sickening, and I would vomit on sight for the smell of it.

I grimaced, washed my face, and cleaned up a bit. I cannot let everyone think that I was pregnant. No, I will not let those thoughts invade my private life.

For all they know, I was *not* married, except for Aleena, because she was my best friend.

I walked out of the restroom before I ventured out to take my case file and the cover that I would have to present to Ashton when he got back. I think he would be furious with me if I were not careful.

Or he would discover something that would make him speechless even more.

I smiled before I thought, thinking of the other agent. I sighed as I looked at the name of the spy that I had to kill to keep my country safe.

Well, I did choose to be their assassin and all of that, so it will be a matter of time to kill whilst one was pregnant.

I took my coat and briefcase before I was out of the building.

"Where are you going?" Aleena asked me.

I smiled at her. I hugged her and told her that I had a mission to go to. She wrinkled her nose, and I knew what she was going to say.

"I know, I know. I will talk to Ashton when he gets back," I said as Aleena scowled at me.

"You better, or *I* will," she said for the last time as I went down to the lobby and called for my car.

I put on my sunglasses before I got into my car and drove back to my house to prepare for the mission to kill one Frederic Rhein.

I PULLED MY STUFF FROM my hiding place around the house. It was neatly arranged, and everything was shiny. I smiled as I took a pistol and a knife before I shoved some money into the duffel bag that I would be carrying to the country where I would be killing the spy. I sighed as I was packing up some of the stuff other than my weapons.

Everything was set and prepped for me. I put on my bodysuit that clung to my body as I was looking at the time. It was 8 in the evening. It was time for me to fly out of the country.

I put my stuff in the boot of my car and went out of the driveway. I sighed as I passed the neighbourhood that we decided to settle in, Ashton and I.

I smiled before I looked ahead toward the mission, which would be the last time for me before I quit for good.

"I WANT YOU TO BE PRECISE. It is simple: get in and get out. But don't get caught," Megan said as I was looking at her across the plane that I would drop from the sky.

The land below was full of fresh water, and I knew that I would have to swim to get into the enemy's territory.

"You know you can count on me, right? I have been doing this forever, Meg," I said as I was strapping myself to the parachute that I would be using.

I put my weapons onto the side of my suit as I was thinking about how to approach the subject of my resignation.

"Megan, I—"

"Here's the dropping point," Megan said.

I sighed. I put on the goggles, and I looked at Megan for the last time as I went to the door.

"Remember, get in, and get out. Do not get caught,"

"Yes, *Mother*," I smirked before I jumped. I was looking at the land that was far below me. I was spreading my hands and legs. I was feeling the breeze that was touching my body.

It used to fill my comfort, but not now. I never thought that I would be worried about dropping into the wrong spot.

I was pushing through the wind, looking at the spot where I would be landing. Then, I pulled the parachute. I was flying in the sky, manoeuvring myself to be unseen until I was inside the territory.

AFTER LANDING, I ABANDONED the parachute and went on for a swim inside the river. The enemy's base was on the other side of the cliff. I was looking for a way in and what could be a better way for me to get inside if I was not looking at the river and got inside from there.

I smirked before I sank under the river. I was swimming toward the cliff. The water was calming, and it was not every day that I got to swim in the river. This trip will be my one-time experience now, for I will never come near this again.

I got up to the side to take some air before I was pushed down into the water again. My hair was floating around the water. I pushed forward.

There was a sewer on the other side of the cliff, and I took one of my tools to get inside. I unlocked the rig, and I was swimming inside.

I got up from the water and looked at the dark alley that was spread thin in front of me. I took a deep breath. I went to the edge and hauled myself up. The water was dripping down on the floor, making wet noises.

I grunted, for I didn't want the enemy to know that I was inside their base. I took out my guns and knives in the places that I could reach.

Then, I was walking silently and quickly on the floor as I was looking out where the enemies might be coming onto me.

And for once, I was not ready to see what was coming at me.

I felt the hair at the back of my nape rising, and before I could do anything, I was hit from behind as I was moving forward. I was looking at the *stiletto* that was walking in front of me.

Then, everything went black.

I BLINKED ONCE. THEN, I blinked again.

I was not in the dirty sewage anymore, for I was hanging at the wall with the chains on my wrists. I tried to tug at them and to prevail, no, for it was tight.

My wrists were hurting me. I cursed in five languages before I took in the place that I am currently located in.

It had a single lamp that was burning my eyes with yellow light, and the room was small. I would say it was a dungeon, but it did not smell bad at all.

Later, I was focused on the door that was in front of me, fourteen feet away, before I took in a deep breath.

Get in, and get out. Do not get caught. Megan warned me about this, and I was too proud to say that she was right. I was careless and looked where it got me.

The door creaked open as I heard the distinctive sound of clicking heels. I knew it was a woman from the silhouette that was coming closer and closer to me. I just don't think it would be a *beautiful* woman.

Blonde hair with grey eyes.

Such wonder.

But I steeled myself, for I knew she might be here to torture me. And I have to be prepared so that I will not be spilling anything at all to her.

Not in my life.

"Well, well, well, looks like you're awake, and here I was thinking of waking you up with a pail of water," she said as she smiled at me. I did not return it.

"Who are you?" I asked her as I was gripping the chains around my wrists. She smirked before she was circling me. Okay, *now* I was feeling uncomfortable.

"You're not that good-looking. I don't even know why *he* chose you. He could have chosen your friend, but no, he had to have *you*," she said before she gripped my chin with her red blood claws.

"But of course, *I* was the real deal anyway. Not you," the villainess, whose name was Tanya, sneered when she released me.

I blinked my eyes at her as if I thought she was insane for talking about something that was not in my context. She laughed.

"Oh, silly me. I know you would not understand this. Perhaps *this* will help," Tanya said as she waved her hand. Something, a *person*, came from the shadows.

I looked at it, and my blood turned to ice when I saw who it was. The blonde woman smiled.

"Now, isn't it just a wonderful *reunion*?" she said as she lay on the chest that I had claimed for a year now.

Ashton—my *husband*—was looking at me with his hazel eyes; it was not from love but from the hatred that I didn't know he possessed.

Chapter 5

"**A**h, I do love a very good story," the woman said as I was looking at my husband. Then, I was looking at her.

"But then, again, I love the *plot twists* more. It was something that I could not think of. Anything would be better when the hero *betrayed* his love interest after all," the woman said. She was looking at Ashton with love. And he did the same.

I felt like a gut was *punched* in my face.

"Now, I will leave you to get the information that I know you will get from her. Have fun," the blonde woman said as she pulled him by the name and kissed him fully.

Ashton was gripping her tiny waist before I turned to look away. I don't think I can stomach this any more than my heart can.

Ashton *betrayed* me. My *husband*, the *love* of my life, betrayed me, and it pierced through my soul.

"I'll see you later, *miene liebe*," Ashton murmured. I rolled my eyes.

The blonde woman looked at me. She smirked and exited the room. The door closed, and I was left with the last person that I would be expecting to see.

The silence was stretching as far as it could be. I sighed and chuckled bitterly.

"So, this is where Fate was telling what a cruel sense of humour it has," I mumbled as I looked at the retreating blonde woman.

Then, I was turning my gaze to look at Ashton. It had been a few days since I had looked at him, and he was still the same husband that I loved.

The *traitor* that I called my husband.

Ashton looked at me. He was looking at my wrists before he was looking at my bodysuit. It clung to my curves, and I was taking a deep breath. My chest was rising and falling before he settled on my face. His hazel eyes were unreadable.

"Is this how you spend your work in the outstation? Filling in people with information as well as warming someone *else*'s bed?" I chuckled before I shook my head.

"I'm a fool," I whispered before Ashton was clearing his throat. I looked at him.

"As much as I want to lie to you, Ashley," he called my name.

No more endearment *liebling* that he always called when we're alone. I guessed that was a lie, after all.

"You can see that you are in a sticky situation, and this time," Ashton stared at me as I focused on his handsome face. "You can never escape," he said as he smirked at me.

I felt a familiar ache inside me as I was concealing my emotions.

Ashton smirked when he was tracing his fingers on my jaws. The gesture was familiar when he used to when we were entangled in bed after making love. I flinched.

"Seeing that you are walking right into our trap, I think it was only a courtesy for me to be *gentle* with you. As long as I got the information that I wanted," Ashton said.

I laughed humorlessly. The sound echoed before I looked at him sharply. I squared my shoulders. Tears were burning my eyes for the fact that I thought he *loved* me as I did for him.

I was wrong, and it was my *first* mistake.

"Try me," I said as I was looking at Ashton. He smirked and leaned closer.

"Oh, believe me, I will, and you will do exactly like I say, Ashley," he said as he stepped back. He was rolling up his sleeves.

I don't know what was about him, but the look that he gave me was murderous.

At that moment, I realized I was not dealing with Ashton Flammen, my husband, whom I have sworn for my life.

No, this was Frederic Rhein, the man that I was supposed to kill. Only *I* was not the one calling the shots.

"Now, we have to check if you're carrying anything that might be used to escape when our backs were turned," Ashton said emotionlessly. He was stepping closer into my personal space.

I was looking up at his handsome face when his hands were roaming my body.

I know he did not mean to do it, for I can see the hatred in his eyes. I felt his hands on my arms, searching for any concealed weapons.

Then, he was putting on my shoulders. I was breathing hard as the hormones were acting up.

Damn it, pregnancy!

Then, his hands strayed down on my chest as I was trying not to arch my back at his touch. I have been waiting for his return, and I don't think that I could ever see anyone else who would be daring to do as such when, clearly, he *hated* me.

Then, his hands were on my bosom. I bit my tongue to let out a moan.

"Well, there were no weapons *here*," he whispered as his hot breaths were on my face. I could smell his minty breaths as I was leaning closer.

Just one kiss, and I can forget him...*forever*.

But Ashton did not stay there as he was kneeling in front of me. He was tracing his hands on my stomach. His hazel eyes were looking at me. I was staring at him stoically before he went on.

He put his hands on my thighs, and I was gulping. Good god! What is *wrong* with me?! He was the enemy, and he would not hesitate to kill me if I was to escape from there.

And here I was, thinking about getting in bed with him!

I am a sick, *sex-deprived* person.

Ashton dragged his hands to my calves before he was patting my behind. He was putting on my buttocks as he got to his feet. He was searching my back.

My bosoms hit his hard chest, and I gasped for a moment. Ashton was arching his eyebrow. I turned away from his gaze before he gripped my nape, and I was forced to look at his handsome face.

The black hair that I gripped whenever I could.

The hazel eyes that I loved so much flared with love for me once upon a time.

The body that belonged to me, and I can seek pleasure and safety in it.

I was looking at his face, trying to memorize all the simple details, and yet it was something that I knew I would always see in my dreams when this was over.

A single *tear* rolled down my cheek.

Ashton stepped back as his face was expressionless. I cannot know what he was thinking when he straightened himself and looked at me for once.

He turned away from me. His back was in my sight as he was walking out of the room.

"Tomorrow, do not expect the same courtesy as you had today," he said softly before he walked out the door.

It slammed shut before I was drowning in my misery, and the tears were rolling down even more as I sobbed over the loss that I don't think I would ever have.

THE NEXT MORNING CAME. My eyes were puffy, and I could not see well in the damn room as I was looking around. I know for sure that my eyes were red as I was crying and sobbing for all the deception that Ashton did.

No, not Ashton. His name is *Frederic*.

I was gripping my hands into fists as I was thinking of one thousand and one ways to kill him. I know that I would not regret it when I had to kill my husband. And *that* was what I would be doing.

Killing him would be easy enough.

As I was contemplating to rip his head off his sinful body, the door opened, and I was looking at the blonde woman and Ashton.

No! Frederic.

"Well, I can see that your method was a success, Fred. You made her cry, and I never thought that you could be so heartless," she said victoriously.

I was looking at her, trying to look for her angle in this sick game of hers.

No, I was a prisoner. A *dangerous* one, yes, but a *helpless* one as well.

"What? No snide remarks?" she asked before she went to the tray that held any kind of torture device. I sensed some shifting, but when I looked, I saw Ashton standing still.

No, Frederic!

"Now, shall we get on with our experiment on your body, Ashley? I know for a fact that you might be an *assassin*, but right now, you're *hopeless*, and your husband," she chuckled when she said that, "was *not* your husband. Ah! What a *dramatic* ending, would you say?" she asked me.

I stayed silent.

The blonde woman tilted her head before she clicked her tongue.

"Very well. Suppose that's how you want to play it. Then, I just have to make do," Tanya said before she took something in her hands. It glittered in the dim light.

My heart started to race. I looked at it, and it was a knife. A small knife but deadly all the same.

"Now, let the fun begin," she said before she slashed my arm, and my screams filled the room.

Chapter 6

I don't know how long I have been here. I don't think I can think correctly right now, for every day and night, I have been tortured by the blonde woman as Ashton was looking from the other side of the room.

I know I should not hope that he would change his mind, but a little part of me, the *hopeful* one, was thinking of convincing him to get out of there and turn his side on his comrades.

But of course, that would be taking life, for if I cannot change him in one year, what will it be for me to change him *forever*?

This enemy was *his* family, and *he* protected them. I was *not* his family. I thought I was when every night he would whisper sweet nothings in my ears, and we would make love to each other.

I thought I had his heart, but the blonde woman was kissing him right now, knowing that *I* was there.

I know the answer to *his* heart.

After every torture that they put on me, I would scream and shout as they would ask questions about the military defences. We had been trained to keep our mouths shut when it was time to surrender.

I did my best in that training because I was an assassin, and I was the one who suggested the training.

But there was a time when I would wish that they would kill me. Bruises were everywhere as my suit was torn, and no one noticed it.

I was whipped, cracked, jabbed, and many more that I didn't know what they were doing.

I was lost, for I was not the controller of my body, and I let my mind wander. Sure, the voices were my own, but I was not in that room at that time.

I was somewhere *safe*, somewhere that I knew I would have my happy ending, somewhere my husband Ashton Flammen was mine and only mine.

Forever.

"Stop," Ashton—*Frederic*—told my torturer as he was instructing something. I don't know what I was doing at the time, for I just surrendered. My eyes were burning with tears, but I didn't shed it.

No one deserved to see it, not even Ashton Flammen slash Frederic Rhein.

"I don't think this will be as efficient as anything else we tried. This wench is a tough cookie,"

I heard every word as I was focusing on the ceiling of the room. But I don't think the enemies know that I was not in the moment as well.

"Leave," Ashton said before the torturer was arching his brows.

"But, sir, milady—"

"She will agree with me, or have you forgotten who the one who warms her bed every night was?" Ashton asked him before the torturer excused himself.

Ashton sighed. He was kneeling in front of me as I was being chained to the ground, knelt to feel the pain in my back.

"Why are you being *difficult*, Ashley? It was *simple*: you just have to tell me *everything* that you know, and you will be *free*," Ashton said as I was coming back to my body now.

I turned my face to look at his face, and I saw that his hazel eyes were holding some emotion in them.

Hatred? Regret? *Longing*? *Yearning*?

Perhaps I don't know what it was, for it was gone when that blonde woman came back into the room.

Ashton turned to look at his beloved before she focused on me.

"What are you doing, Fred?" she asked curiously. Ashton stood up, and I was looking at his long legs that were going to the woman.

No, not *this* torture. I could not bear it when Ashton was kissing another woman.

Another woman that *he* loved so much more than *me*.

The tears were rolling down now as the woman turned to look at me again. She smirked when she was pulling Ash by his nape and kissed him.

They were kissing sloppily. I could hear the noise and the moans that the lady released from her mouth. I wanted to smack her, and I tried to kill her.

But first, I have to get to her.

The lady stopped kissing Ashton. Then, she went to kneel in front of me. My eyes were tracing her body.

She smirked at me and traced her hands on my face. I flinched before I leaned back.

"Ah, are you *finally* ready to spill your tea, Ashley? It wasn't difficult to say when your heart was so on display for everyone to *manipulate*," she said as she looked at Ash. He leaned against the walls now.

"And it was never a good thing for the enemy to know your *weakness*, doesn't it?" she said before I turned to look at her face.

She was pretty for a villainess, but I don't want to say that out loud.

I took a deep breath as I was looking at the ground. I have to time it right before I can strike and when I can take Tanya by surprise.

She was near me now, and I was looking at her. I smiled as I stared into her hateful face, and I knew I would enjoy the killing later.

Just bidding my timing, after all.

"Well, you're right. I have a weakness that you can use and manipulate at your fingertips," I said as my eyes drifted to Ashton. He stilled.

"But you also show your weakness today, lady," I said as I was smirking at her. She arched her eyebrow.

"*This*," I said as I head-butted her, and the crack was sounding across the room.

I laughed before I flipped her, and I was on top of her as far as the chains let me. I smacked her ribs, and she was grunting with pain.

"How's this for your torture, *wench*?" I said when someone was gripping my arms from behind. The blonde woman shoved me off. I was trying to get out of the hold that locked me in.

"Control yourself,"

It was Ashton. He did not want me to kill his stupid wench.

"Let *me* go," I hissed before the blonde lady took something from the tray. Her eyes became murderous. I was screaming and shouting when something was embedded into my stomach.

No!

My eyes widened as I looked at the woman who was pushing the blade into my stomach to its hilt. The lady smirked at me before Ashton released me. The blood was pooling in front of me as it slid down my suit.

"No," I whispered as I knelt on the floor and I was gripping the blade. Then, I took it out as I shouted. It was deafening before I was trying to stop the bleeding.

"If you think that you ever had the upper hand *here*," the blonde woman spat at my face as she was gripping my hair. I was wailing now for the pain of the wound on my stomach.

But it was for my *unborn* child. The child that I promised to tell my husband after his outstation.

And now, all of them were gone in a glimpse.

Those memories of us together in a suburban neighbourhood and the family that we will *eventually* build.

Gone, turned into dust.

"You might want to think again," she said before she put another blade, and I cried.

I was crying now, for I knew my baby would never survive if I were bleeding to death. I was sobbing when the blonde woman was removing herself from the room, smirking as she did so.

"Let's go. Let the wench *bleed* to death for all I care," she said as I was trying to stop my bleeding.

I was wailing before my eyes burned with my hot tears. Then, everything that was focused on me was *Ashton*.

The *traitor* husband of mine.

"*Please*," I said as I was trying to get the words out of my throat. I needed to tell Ashton the truth.

The truth was that what I spent with him for a year has resulted in this. This *pregnancy* was his legacy that I would carry despite the change that has happened between us.

"*I love you*, Ashton," I whispered as Ashton stiffed. I can see his shoulders tensed as I was putting those words.

"Even if you hate me so much, would you hate *your* child even more?" I said as Ashton stared at me. His eyes were indifferent.

"Even when I die, save him or her. Save our *child*, please," I said before I lay on the ground, feeling the blood coming from the wounds.

I caressed my stomach as Ashton was looking at the movement of my hand. He smirked.

"Then, I suggest you kill the bastard before it comes into this world," he walked back out of the room. Hatred was flaring into his eyes.

"For you're sure to know how to act sweet and innocent when I know that you're a *she-devil*," Ashton said with disgust.

I was closing my eyes, prayers on my lips as the darkness was coming to claim me.

At last, I will feel the peace that I have been searching for when I was captured in the enemy's hand on day one.

Chapter 7

I did not know what had happened, for I blacked out when the blood kept coming out of my stomach. I begged for Ashton to help our child, but he dumped me.

He dumped the love that I was sharing with him. Tears were burning inside my eyes before I tossed on my side.

I was on a bed. I realized that now, for it was soft like a marshmallow underneath me. I slowly opened my eyes. I looked around, taking in the sight that I was in.

I was not in the torture room anymore, for I was on a bed, the covers were covering my body. I sat up as I noticed that someone had bandaged my stomach and the wounds from the knives.

"Ah, you're awake," the feminine sound was coming from behind me.

I turned and looked at the old woman who smiled at me. I don't know what about her I was comfortable with, but I must be wary.

I cannot afford any mess more than I was already in.

I was looking at the old woman. I don't know if she was a cruel person because she was in this territory. However, my instinct told me that she was *nice*.

At least she helped me recover fully from bleeding out to die.

"Where am I?" I asked her. My voice hoarse. I don't know how many days it has been since I last opened my eyes.

And by the looks of it, it had been a while since my voice was coarse, and I was thirsty as hell.

"Here," she said before she handed me a glass of water, which I emptied in seconds. I was asking for another one, and she gave it to me. Sweet, *sweet* water, for I longed for it when I was in the torture room.

"Easy, your stomach is empty. We need to get you some food," the old woman said before she pushed a button.

I didn't want to know what she did because my stomach was growling loudly as I was holding it.

Then, the question was upon me.

I looked at the old woman as she was shuffling around. I don't know how to approach the subject of my pregnancy.

Did Ashton order her to kill the baby? Did I lose it in the bleeding? So many possibilities that can only mean *one* thing.

My baby was *dead*.

Realizing that I was silent, the old woman turned to look at me as I was staring at her back. She smiled and noticed my hand on my stomach before she sighed.

"It was tough luck. Your baby was still intact, and you're not causing any more trouble than it should. You're lucky you do not have a miscarriage," the old woman explained as I was blinking my eyes.

My baby was safe. *Safe.*

I sighed as I slouched a bit, but reality hit me like a storm. I know that I will never be safe. Not when I was still trapped in here. I have to get out. I just have to.

"Is there any way—"

"I cannot help you more than I could, lady. I was instructed to treat you, but if I help you escape, my family will be dealt with," the old woman said before her face turned solemn.

I looked at the ground as the heavy silence was between us. The healer sighed when I was looking at her old face again.

"Who's the father?" she asked before I was taken aback with her question. Then, I remembered that we were in the parts of the world where they don't accept a child out of wedlock. Good thing I was married then.

An ache tugged inside my heart.

"He's...away. But I assure you he's my *husband*," I said, not knowing why I should explain myself to this woman. Perhaps it was the look in her eyes that made me want to tell her everything.

How my marriage was a *lie*, the love of my life turned out to be *someone else* who *used* me, and the family that I have been dreaming of will never come true now.

So much that I wanted to tell her, and the burning of the tears inside my eyes was all I could think about. I blinked them away.

No need to waste any tears over spilt milk now.

"Thank you," I said honestly. The old woman stopped. Then, she resumed again, tidying up her stuff before she went to the door.

She reached for the doorknob but hesitated for a moment, perhaps wanting to tell me something. I cannot read her like a book.

"That man, the one that brought you in for treatment, was *he* the father?" she asked slowly. I blinked my eyes. I looked at her before I nodded slowly.

As far as I'm concerned, Ashton was the only male in this territory. The old woman nodded.

"He was distressed when you're bleeding out. Perhaps *all* was not lost yet," the healer said in a whisper, but I heard it loud and clear because of my impeccable hearing.

Ashton...*worried* about me? Well, that's a new one, for I thought he never cared about me, even with our marriage.

"Please restrain yourself from doing anything dangerous. You don't want to have a miscarriage," the old woman said softly. She went out of the room, leaving me alone with the thought that I never believed it before. Not until now.

Aston Flammen—no, Frederic Rhein—worried about me? His target?

Well, that was *something* that I could use to my advantage.

I DON'T KNOW WHAT TIME it was, but I can assume that it was an evening for Ashton, who was walking inside the room with a tray that smelled like food. And my stomach grumbled as I was looking at his handsome face.

The black hair and hazel eyes. Oh, how I wished to capture it and gripped it.

However, that would be a lie, for I know that *he* was the enemy. My heart refused to see it.

"Eat," he instructed when I was looking at him. He was arching his eyebrow at me as I was still like a stone on the bed.

"Come on, Ashley, eat. You need your strength," he said as if he was desperate for me to eat.

Maybe what the old woman said was true after all.

Ashton might be a *lying, conniving* bastard that I have to kill, but if there was a small amount of worry for *me*...

I think I cannot kill him if I wanted to later on. And so, I locked away my feelings as I was looking at the tray warily.

"If I wanted you dead, I would leave you to bleed. So, do not worry about the food that might be poisoned. I cooked these meals *myself*," Ashton said before I snapped my eyes at him.

I blinked. I never thought that Ashton could cook for one year, and we stayed together under the pretence that he loved me; I was always the one who did the cooking.

Perhaps I don't know the *real* Ashton Flammen after all—or Frederic Rhein, for that matter.

"Please eat," he said quietly before I sighed. Then, I went to the tray and opened the lid. And smelled that *wretched* scent.

Ginger, of all things.

My stomach revolted at the smell. I was gripping my mouth as the bile was coming up to my mouth. I saw a door that led to the bathroom before I was running toward it.

I shoved the lid of the toilet up before I was vomiting the contents of my empty stomach. I clutched the side of the bowl when someone was pulling my hair away from the bathroom.

A warm hand was massaging me up and down as I was pushing the content out of my body. Tears were burning in my eyes as I knew that this was too good to be true. They needed me as a *prisoner*, so Ashton did what he thought was right.

I cannot be swayed by his kindness now.

I heaved and heaved as I was breathing hard. The bitter smell of my vomit was filling the room. I pulled the flush.

The water swirled. I was taking a deep breath as I was feeling the warm sensation on my neck.

Ashton was breathing hard behind me.

I looked at him over the shoulder before he composed himself. He stood up and put some distance between us. I pushed myself to stand up on my own feet. Ashton cleared the throat.

"Eat, and I'll come back later to take the tray," he said, moving out of the bathroom. I stopped him as I asked him to remove the ginger-smelling food.

He nodded and took it with him before I went to eat the food. My stomach growled. I sighed as I devoured the food.

I did not know that I was *starving*, and right now, I don't care about anything else.

Perhaps one of the perks of being pregnant was that I had a big appetite as big as an elephant.

I rolled my body on the mattress after I set the tray down. Then, exhaustion was coming onto me. I closed my eyes, and sleep came over me.

I don't know if it was a dream or not. But someone was playing with my hair. I leaned into the touch that warmed my heart as I heard something surreal.

"You will always be *my* choice, Ashley, for you have *ensnared* me on that day in the bar," Then, a kiss on my forehead as I was slipping away into the abyss again.

Chapter 8

Well, perhaps my wish was too much when I was transferred back to the torture room. I thought I was making some progress, but of course, that *wench*, the blonde woman, was making it difficult for me to escape.

And to think that I could sway Ashton to be on my side.

I sighed as the chains around my wrists were clacking against the wall. Then, the room was opened, and the blonde woman and Ashton were revealed in tow.

"Ah, I see that you're not bleeding, and I can torture you even more," she said before I glared at her.

Seriously, I would kill her the first thing after I escape this mess. But for now, play like a dumb doe.

"Fred told me that it will be no use for us if you're dead. And we still need that information for your military secret. My love," she said as she was extending her arm, asking Ashton to pick a torture device from the tray.

Ashton picked up something, and it was a flogger. She grimaced.

"My love, I don't think—"

"She is still recovering, and we don't want the villagers to suspect that we were killing people here. Good thing that old woman did not say anything after treating her," Ash said logically while the blonde woman grimaced.

However, she agreed anyway. She shrugged before she raised the flogger, and I was waiting for the torture to come.

Then, I only heard my screams.

I WAS LEANING AGAINST the wall as I was looking at the room. I was back in the torture room, but this time with a loose chain that I could move around with. But not close enough to get to the door, and I was sitting too far from the tray to get something from it.

Yes, they have given me some space for me to walk and perhaps do some exercise. I don't know who influenced who, but if I have to guess, it was Ashton.

Ashton the traitor.

I sighed before I leaned against the wall as I closed my eyes. I took a deep breath when the door opened, meaning that my evening meal was here. It was usually one of the guards that were coming in.

But *tonight*, it was Ashton.

I stepped back as I was leaning even more against the wall when he put the tray on the floor. He was looking at me, wanting me to approach the meal before he could get out of the room.

"Are you going to go now?"

"Are you going to eat now?"

I grimaced. I stepped forward and pulled the tray onto my lap. It was soup with hot bread tonight. The soup was chicken soup, and my mouth watered at the sight. Then, I dug in, not caring that Ashton was looking at me with his hazel eyes.

"You've lost weight," he said as a matter of fact. I rolled my eyes. I stuffed even more bread into my mouth.

"Of course, I would. When you're a prisoner, you don't get much choice in the food department," I said with my mouth full of food.

Ashton was grimacing at me. I shrugged as I sipped on the soup. It was delicious, and I bet my life that Ashton was cooking it.

"Will you ever give the secret?" he asked quietly after he took a seat on the floor.

My hands were still on the glass containing water. I sipped it. I cleared my throat as I was putting the tray aside before I regarded my husband.

Well, *ex-husband* after this.

"I don't think you would give the information even when your life was on the line," Ashton said, making me roll my eyes at him.

"Then you know that you will waste your time to convince me to give it up," I said as I was looking at him now.

Ashton smirked. His hazel eyes shone with mischief.

"And why do you think that I would even ask for it? You know I can get the information for the last year that we were together," he said before I was clenching my jaws.

The year where I gave my *love* to him only to have him stab me in the back. The bloody bastard.

"Right, the year where I thought I was going to build a family with you, but it turns out you're *not* even thinking about it," I whispered before I was looking at the ground. Ashton sucked on his breaths.

"Ashley, I—"

"Get out. I don't want to see your face. Just let me be miserable *alone* here," I said when my tears were in my eyes.

Stupid hormones. Why does it have to do something that I don't want to show my weakness to Ashton right now?

The silence was deafening, and he did not even move. I sighed before I looked at him. I was stunned by the emotions that were playing in his eyes. Then, my husband looked away.

"Are you even going to tell me that you're *pregnant*?" he asked quietly.

I was biting my lower lips. I was supposed to be talking about this when we had our chance, but then he had to go, and now the truth came out.

Everything was a *mess*. My life, my husband, my secret...

I don't think that my life would be this complicated when I lay with him for the first time that night after our banter. I sighed.

"Ashton, I—"

"So, you don't even consider to tell *me*?" he asked again. Ashton laughed bitterly as he rubbed his mouth. I bit my lips.

"No, of course not. I was thinking of talking to you about it when you're back from your job, but apparently, *that* will never happen again. For I am doomed to be here and die with this...child of mine," I said the last one quietly, knowing that Ash did not want it.

He did suggest aborting our child.

"You think I would not—"

I snapped my eyes to him, feeling the anger inside me. He knew that he was suggesting that I would get an abortion.

Now, he was trying to get my heart wound up again. I stood up and sized him up. I was gritting my teeth.

"This is the proof that my love was *real*, even when you're dallying with your...*woman*. I know that I am only a target for you to sleep and perhaps play with my emotions, but know this, Ashton Flammen or Frederic Rhein." I said with a chill in my voice.

"My love was *real*, and with that, I decided to show it to the world when this baby came into the world. If he survived," I said as the tears were free-flowing now.

I could not stop the sob that was coming from me, knowing that I would be left alone to nurture this love, *our* love.

And I would be proud to do it even when my husband thinks *otherwise*.

I was about to tell him more about my decision when Ashton pulled me into his arms and kissed me.

I gasped, not knowing what was going on until my body yielded to his desire. *Lust* and *want*. I could not deny it either, for every time I saw him, my heart beat faster, and I could not seem to contain my eagerness when Ashton would look my way and see who I was.

The *real* me.

I moaned when Ashton was pushing me against the wall, hooking his arms around my knees. He was grinding himself to me. I was arching my back as I was gripping his hair. It has been too damn long since I have him in my arms.

And I was *aching* for it.

"*Ashton*," I whispered as he was kissing my jaws and throat. I moaned even more before his hands were fumbling with my suit and unzipped it.

I was wet in my nether mouth, for I was breathing hard when those hazel eyes were focusing on me. I was fumbling with his belt when I was unzipping his pants and pulling them down his thighs.

His erected cock sprang free as I was gripping it in my hands. Ashton hissed softly. He was kissing me again. His tip was at my entrance.

"Even with everything that happened, I still want you, Ashley Banner, and you want me, too," he whispered before he slammed into me.

I arched my back even more as the chains were rattling. Ashton was pumping in and out of my core as I was gripping his hair while his tongue was on my nipples.

"*Ashton*," I moaned his name when he was increasing his tempo. Being pregnant has its perks, as I was easily aroused, and Ashton was making me aroused with desire for him even more.

I was wrapping my legs around his torso and pushing my heels into his buttocks. I was kissing his neck, and I bit down, not enough to draw blood, but it would leave a hickey tomorrow.

"*Ashley*," Ashton moaned, feeling the desire between us even though we were supposed to be enemies.

Perhaps the forbidden love was making it even *tastier* and *sweeter* than anything.

I was moving in sync with him, and before I knew it, the stars exploded. I was screaming his name at the top of my lungs.

"*Liebling*,"

It just came out like when we're used to it. I know I shouldn't call it, but my heart was having a hard time recognizing that Ashton was my enemy. And I was *his*.

But what could a woman in love like me think when my husband was ravishing me as he *starved* for it? I could not just let this feeling go, for I was desperate for it as well.

I guessed we're well-matched, after all, blurring the lines between lust and love for a forbidden love that would never blossom into anything else.

Well, except the baby that was growing inside me to be the proof of our romance to each other, no matter what people say about it.

Chapter 9

And later that night, Ashton was ravishing me again and again as I was allowing him to. This night was our *goodbye*, the last time that we would see each other before we had to kill.

Only one will survive, and I know that I will not be the person to call the shots.

I was a *captive*, after all.

We were at it as if the world was going to end tomorrow. No more pretence, no more inhibitions.

Ashton showed me what he wanted to do to do with his tongue, fingers, and cock. I cannot deny it, for I loved and longed for it. I just had to live without it when this was all over.

But the thing was, I didn't want this to be over—*whatever* it was between us. Plus, Ashton was spending his night in my room, and he hugged me like he could not let me go.

We were snuggling against the cold floor as our clothes were discarded. I don't want to sleep, for I know that Ashton will leave me on my own.

And I don't want him to.

We were in comfortable silence as if we could hear the needle drop on the floor. It was too much for me to bear when I cleared my throat first.

"Well, this is *unexpected*," I said as I was looking at his handsome face. Ashton clenched his jaws. I can see the tension in his shoulders. I reached out, but he was already moving out of my touch.

Out of *our* love nest.

"This is a mistake," he mumbled, but I heard him loudly and clearly. I was gulping, for I knew that he would not betray his comrades for me. I know this, but my heart was still hoping that he would reconsider.

"Ashton—"

"My name is *not* Ashton. My name is Frederic, and you better start using it, Ashley,"

His words stung, and I dropped my hand from reaching him. I hugged myself as I knew that he would be cold again, and I had to prepare myself for this.

Ashton was rubbing his face now as I was blinking away my tears.

"I'm sorry," I said before he stilled. So, I continued.

"I'm sorry if my love *burdened* you then and now. I know you will never feel the same. And I know that you will have to leave," I was sobbing now as the tears were coming down my face.

"I just wished that you would be happy with whoever you love, Fred—"

"Do not use *that* name," Ash said as he was gripping my face.

I was looking at him through the blurry eyes. His hazel eyes were focusing on my emerald ones. I blinked before he sighed.

"I'll always be Ashton to *you*, Ashley," he said when I sobbed now. He was saying goodbye, and I knew it, but then, he said something *else* that made my heart jump.

"And I will get you out of *here*,"

I snapped my eyes to him. I blinked my eyes when he smirked. He kissed me, and I was still stunned to look at him.

"What?"

"You would think I let my *wife* die here? I think you don't know me at all," Ashton said before he dressed up and urged me to do so. I was still confused by this sudden change in his behaviour.

"What are you playing at?" I asked him.

Ashton was looking at me. I was still naked, and he was helping me to get the clothes on me.

"We have to escape first. I don't think Megan will forgive me if anything happens to her assassin." He said before I was blinking my eyes.

What the *hell* was going on?

Seeing the confusion on my face, Ashton kissed me before he spoke.

"Later, I will explain it later. For now," Ashton said as I heard a bomb going off. He smirked.

"Let's get out of here,"

ASHTON LED ME OUT OF the room, where everyone was screaming and shouting in the distance. I don't know what to expect, but Megan was sending him to infiltrate this territory, and he was on my side all along, or I was being *duped* by him and trusting him like my heart wanted me to.

But do you even want to stay behind without him in your life? I don't have an answer for that either.

We were running through the long hallway when I saw who was blocking us. It was the blonde woman, and she was looking from me to Ashton before smirking.

"Well, I have always known it would come to this. I or your wife, and you chose *her*," Tanya said with disdain. She was removing the *blades* that she carried. I don't even know how she walked with it all the time.

"Let us through, and nobody will get hurt," Ashton said.

I was gripping his hand. I looked at him briefly, noticing that his jaws were clenching. Then, I looked at the woman again. She laughed.

"I think it was too late for *that*," she said as she was moving forward as quickly as a cheetah.

Ashton shoved me to the side before he met that woman with blades of his own. How does *he* get that?

"Move aside. Stand down," Ash said as he was swinging the blades, bringing terror into the hallway. But the blonde woman only laughed, and she was sneering at him.

"Not a chance. Not after you broke your oath," she hissed before she was slicing Ashton.

My husband grunted as I was standing in horror. His sword flew away as the woman was holding the tip of her sword at his throat. Then, she looked at me and smirked.

"Say goodbye forever, *wench*," she said, and then, something snapped at me. I took the blade that Ashton threw to the side. I rolled as I was coming upon the woman.

She was punching through my husband's throat when I swiped the sword aside, and I was locking my eyes with her. She was shocked to see me there.

"You–"

"You thought you would kill my *husband*? I think you need to brush up on your swordsmanship," I said before I knocked her down.

She was screaming with rage as I parried her and thrust forward. The blonde woman staggered back. She hit the wall, and I was plunging the sword into her chest. She gasped before blood was oozing from her mouth.

"That's for *kissing* my husband and *torturing* me, *wench*," I said before I released the hilt of the sword and staggered.

So much for showing the art of killing, I think I opened some of the wounds now.

"Come on," Ashton said as he gripped my waist, and we walked down the hallway. He turned before the garden greeted us, and there was someone out there who was waiting for us.

The old woman who treated me days ago.

"Took you long enough," she said, sounding not old at all. Then, she peeled her skin, and I was greeted by someone with whom I was familiar. I blinked.

"Aleena?" I asked, and I could not believe it!

My best friend was here. She smiled at me before helping Ashton carry me out of the building.

"How—what—I don't understand," I said as we were running from the burning building.

Does this mean that I was not alone all this time, and Megan found it hilarious that I was captured and had decided to abandon me?

I think I will talk with her.

We were running as the Ash and the debris were flying in the sky. The smoke thickened, and I was coughing.

Then, we're at the cliff that I was looking down on, the freshwater of the river, the same one that I came through on the first day.

"Jump!" Ashton said when he was pulling me with him. I jumped into the river, trusting him with my life.

Aleena was following him as well. We were plunged into darkness before I was swimming to the surface.

My face broke the surface, and I took a deep breath. I coughed some of the water as I was looking at the burning facilities.

Then, we were moving toward the alcove before I saw something on the surface that was crashing with the water.

"A *boat*? So you have an *escape* plan, after all?" I asked them, but Aleena and Ashton were busy trying to start the engine, so they went out of the alcove.

I was looking at the burning building that was sending smoke into the air. I was sure that Megan would know about this sooner or later.

My guess would be *sooner*.

I looked at my husband and best friend. They planned something, and they had to disguise themselves so that I could not think of anything else.

Megan was playing me, and it's time for *payback*.

Chapter 10

I burst into the room as Megan was looking up from her paperwork. I was furious that I didn't want to think about anything else but *her*.

Yeah, that's right. It was time for me to end this bullshit once and for all.

"Well, it looks like you have come back from hell, Ashley," she said as she pulled her glasses from her nose.

I was breathing hard as I asked Ashton and Aleena to bring me to the headquarters first thing when we were in the city.

"You *lied* to me," I said as I was fuming with anger. The hormones were acting up, but I didn't care, for it nearly got me killed last time when Megan withdrew some information that she might share with me.

"I did not lie, Ashley," she said as she was looking at me before she sighed.

"I just withdrew the information so that your emotions will not control you," she said as I was gripping my hands into fists.

"That's even *worse*," I barked before Megan just arched her eyebrow.

"Is it? Or are you mad that your *best friend* was in the game and you're not? I cannot afford to lose the information about our military defence. We can't let them have it," she said before I crossed my hands in front of my chest.

"And you think by not telling me, I would be easily manipulated?" I asked her. I laughed in her face.

"I thought we were *friends*," I mumbled as I looked at Megan. My anger returned.

"But it would seem that I was the only one that felt that way," I said.

I took my weapons and set them on her desk. She knew what I was trying to do, and she did not forbid me from doing it. I cannot hold it together anymore.

Not with this pregnancy and my husband, who did not love me. Perhaps this was my ending, for I was sure I was destined to be *alone* forever.

Assassin or not.

"I'm done," I said as I put my last weapon on the desk. Megan just arched her eyebrow. She stared at me.

"Then, you know what you have to do," she said. I was leaning forward to see Megan eye to eye level.

"Gladly," I said before I took the pill from her hand and took it. I know what I was asking for, and this time, no one will change my mind ever again.

Not Ashton, not Aleena. And *certainly* not Megan.

"Have a nice life, Megan," I said before I swallowed the pill, and everything went blank.

I DID NOT KNOW WHAT had happened. My eyes were heavy, and my back was suffering. I groaned.

I tossed and turned as I looked at the unfamiliar house that was in my surroundings.

I blinked as the curtains were swayed by the breeze of the ocean that I could hear from outside.

"Where am I?" I asked when someone was rasping at the door. I turned to look who it was, and it was someone that I didn't know.

His black hair and hazel eyes were staring at me as he was leaning against the door frame. I was gripping the blanker, for I was in a room with a stranger.

"Yes?" I asked him as he was turning to look at my face.

There was something familiar about him, but I didn't know what it was. So, I did what I always did whenever I was in a difficult situation.

I blurted out the question that was lingering in my mind.

"Are you my kidnapper?" I asked him before his eyes went big as a saucer.

Then, he smiled before he shook his head. He cleared his throat as he took a step forward into the room.

"Please don't hurt me," I added as the man was tilting his head to the side. Looking at me curiously as if I had swallowed something strange.

Perhaps I did, but I am not sure now.

"Ashley, do you know who I am?" he asked. His baritone voice was hitting in the places that I didn't know I wanted to acknowledge.

But yes, his voice was making me shiver in a good way. I wanted his voice to wrap me in his cocoon.

If I knew who *he* was.

"Ashley, it's me. Your husband, Ashton?" he asked me when my head was pounding. I put my fingers to my temples as if something was trying to resurface, but nothing.

Ashton? That sounded *familiar*.

"I...I...I can't be sure now," I said as I turned to look at the mattress that I was sitting on.

The blanket was covering my body. I could sense that I was wearing a nightgown underneath it.

I sighed before I turned to look at the handsome stranger. He slumped at my declaration.

"I see," he said quietly before he cleared his throat and looked at me. Ashton smiled.

"I get the breakfast for you. You must be hungry," Ashton said before he closed the door.

I was left alone; confusion was inside my head, but my heart was beating as if I wanted to go after him.

What is the matter with me?

ASHTON WAS BACK IN the room as he set the tray in front of me. I was still wary of him as I was leaning against the headboard. Ashton was pouring the orange juice into the glass and handed it to me.

"Orange juice?" he asked, and I took it from his hand.

Our fingers touched, and the electricity made me shiver. Ashton turned to look at me, but I brushed the feeling away.

"Here, you should get some food into you. You look thin," Ashton said as he was putting some bacon and sausages on my plate as I was looking at the omelette. My stomach growled, and I was blushing, for this stranger was smirking at me.

"Well, have at it," he said before I picked up the fork and took some of the food.

I brought it to my mouth, and I ate it, looking at Ashton as I chewed them. He was sipping on the orange juice and smacked his lips.

It was glistening with the juice, and my core was *wet* at the sight.

Ashton took some sausage and ate them. I was looking at the mouth, the sensual mouth that I wanted to kiss so badly, as I was slowly eating my breakfast.

We were in comfortable silence before everything was burning inside me. I wanted Ashton so badly that I ached. Then, *I* took the step.

I pushed the tray off the bed before I pulled Ashton by his collar. He was surprised before I claimed his mouth.

I don't care if he was a stranger or someone that I have to be wary of. But my core was *aching*, and I knew *he* could subdue it.

"*Hmm*," he groaned before he was pushing me on the bed. The tray was sprawling on the floor as I was kissing him fervently.

Ashton was roaming my body with his calloused, rough hands before I broke the kiss as he kissed my throat.

"*Ashley*," he said my name as if I was someone *special*. I don't know what was happening, but I know that Ashton belonged to me.

We belonged *together*.

"*Ashton*," I moaned before he was ripping my nightgown. I was ripping his shirt off as I was touching the hard chest underneath my palms.

Ashton groaned before I looked into his eyes. He was looking at me with a painful expression on his face.

"What is it?" I asked him when Ashton climbed off me. I looked at his back as he was rubbing his face with his hands.

"Ashton?"

"I'm sorry. I cannot do this," Ashton said before he was about to flee.

However, I grabbed his wrists and pulled him back into the mattress. I was straddling his hips before some images flashed in front of my eyes.

The burning. The terror. The torture and the screaming. Ashton kissed *someone* that I wanted to rip her head off.

I gasped before I looked at him. Ashton was gripping my waist as I was pushing at his shoulders.

"You...you..."

"I know that you will never forgive me, Ashley. For everything that I have done to you and all the things that happened. But I cannot forget you, and I know that you will never want someone like me to be your husband—"

Everything was silent as I kissed him again. I was looking at his face when I broke it. The tears were dripping down my cheeks.

"Oh, Ashton. *I love you*. And *nothing* can take me away from you. I know you're not perfect, and I don't ask you to be so, but I want you to know that *I love you*, no matter what you think," I said as I caressed his cheeks.

Ashton's eyes glistened with tears before he hugged me, and we held each other.

I remembered, despite the pill that I took, I remembered that Ashton was my husband.

Even in pretence, I knew that my love for him was real. And he was trying to make sure that I would accept him no matter what happened.

"And I love you, Ashley Banner. There's no one for me but *you*," he said as he pulled me by the nape into a kiss that was sweet and tender.

Like *his love* for me.

Epilogue

Ashton pushed me as I was hitting the mattress. After everything that we have been through, I don't think I would let Ashton out of my life. I wanted him forever, and I know that I will be his forever.

Because I love him so much that I cannot let him go.

"Ashton," I moaned as I was gripping his hair. I was arching my back when he was kissing my chest. His tongue—his *wicked, sensual* tongue—was making some wicked things on my nipples. I moaned his name.

"*You're mine*, Ashley. You have always been mine when I was not even sure of myself, and when I know that you are carrying my child, you are mine...*forever*," he said huskily.

I was moaning and aching for him. I wrapped my legs around his torso, and I pulled his hair before I kissed him again.

I was grinding myself to his erection before his tip was teasing me. My core was wet and ready for him as Ashton impaled himself into me. I gasped as I was writhing underneath him.

"*Oh*," I moaned when I was moving in sync with him. I don't know where he began, and I ended. We were joined as one, and as one, we will be together forever.

"*Ashley*," my husband moaned my name as I was moving in sync with him. He was groaning under his breath.

Suddenly, I was feeling the familiar sensation as my walls clenched involuntarily around his cock. I gasped for air. His name was on my lips as I climaxed.

"*Ashton!*"

He nuzzled my neck as he was spewing his hot load into me. It was delicious, and I don't think that I would have been happier without Ashton's arms around me.

"I love you, Ashley Banner, *forever, liebling*,"

"And I am to you, Ashton Flammen, *miene liebe*," I said before he smirked.

"I think I want my surname to be yours. So that we can be together without the government coming after me," Ashton said. I was rolling my eyes.

"Prick,"

"But you love me anyway," he said as he was nudging me again. He was hard inside me. I was narrowing my eyes at him.

"Bastard," I said huskily. Ashton laughed and kissed me again.

And it was *paradise*.

DESPITE EVERYTHING that we've been through, Megan was kind enough to make my existence a ghost.

And right now, I cannot think of anything else, for Ashton was standing beside me. He was putting his hand on my lower back as Megan was arching her eyebrow at me.

"So, I see the rumour was true now," she said. I was rolling my eyes as I was crossing my hands in front of my chest.

"And *whose* fault was that?" I asked her before Ashton warned me. I know that I should not let the anger get to me, but the hormones were overwhelming today. I sighed.

"Look, I know that you don't want to let me go, but I am tired of everything, Megan. I want to have my own family and spend my time with my children. And I have a husband now," I said as I was turning to look at Ash. He smiled as I was biting my lower lips. Megan cleared her throat.

"So, I assume that you are trying to leave us for good then?" she asked before I shrugged. She sighed as she was pinching her nose bridge.

"Well, that makes two of my best agents," she mumbled. Instantly, I perked up and was curious about the other agent.

"Who was it?" I asked her without having thoughts of anything else. Megan looked at me before she smiled.

"You know *who*," she said before she waved her hand at me.

"Go now, make your own family, and I hope that I will be named your child's godmother?" she asked me before I was arching my brows.

"You meant to—"

"I may have been strict with you, Ashley, but remember that I am still a woman with a maternal instinct," she said before she looked at her paper, her subtle way to dismiss the conversation.

I was arching my eyebrow. I turned with Ashton to get out of the office and out of this dangerous life forever.

"Well, *that* went well," he said as we were inside the car. I sighed as I was gripping his hand.

I was looking at the building one last time. I smiled, for I know I would never be here if not for Megan, no matter what she did to me in the past.

"Yeah, I think it is," I said when Ashton drove away from the parking lot to our next destination to ensure that nothing was bad happening to our unborn child.

It's time for my appointment with an OBGYN.

THE LIGHTS WERE BLINDING as I was lying down on the bed. The young doctor was scanning my stomach, looking for signs that my unborn child would be in any danger of some sort when I was being tortured during my capture.

There was none.

"Well, it would seem that everything was okay and your baby is healthy. But I do suggest you take care of your health, ma'am. You're too thin," the doctor said before she looked at me sternly. I smiled.

"I will," I said as Ashton helped me to get out of bed. The doctor was typing something inside the computer.

She was describing some medicine for me so that I would not be having issues before I had my next appointment with her next month.

"Thank you," Ashton said as we exited the room. I was taking a deep breath before I stared at my husband.

The traitor husband that once I knew, but now, he was my world.

We walked in the hallway as the sanitary smell of the hospital was sticking to our clothes like glue.

I was holding Ashton's hand as he led me outside. The sun was shining, and I took a deep breath as I closed my eyes.

"So, what do we do now?" he asked me as I looked at my husband. My only husband, Ashton Banner, is not officially yet.

"Shall we go to the city hall to change your name *officially*?" I asked him.

Ashton was smirking at me. Then, he pulled me in for a kiss.

"I thought you never ask," he whispered as his kiss was taking me to another level.

I WAS BREATHLESS AS Ashton was lying on his back next to me. After we visited the city hall, we rushed home because I could not keep my hands to myself.

I was happy as Ashton had shown me one thought and one way to be wicked with my body.

And I loved every second of it.

"What are you thinking about, *liebling*?" he asked me as he was kissing my bare shoulder.

I was admiring the engagement and wedding rings that I put even after what happened between us. I know that some people might condemn it, for I was sleeping with the enemy.

But Ashton was *my* enemy, and now, he is my husband more than anything.

"Just thinking about our future," I whispered as I turned to snuggle against his warmth.

If anything, I gave Ashton a point for being the cosiest arms in the world. And I loved every second of it, for it was exclusive only for me.

"*Hmm*, and what is our future foretell you?" Ashton asked me as he was tracing his hands on my bare spine.

I sighed. Then, I was kissing Ashton's bare chest. His scent was overwhelming my nostrils, but I loved everything about Ashton Banner.

My Ashton Banner.

"That we will have everything that we could ever dream for. A house, children, pets if we want," I said as I was sitting on my elbow.

Ashton smiled at me with his hazel eyes shining with mischief.

"And you're at my beck and call whenever, wherever I want," he said before he pulled my nape and kissed me. I melted against his hard body before Ashton broke the kiss.

"I have news for you," he said as I was arching my eyebrow at him.

"Okay, what is it about?" I asked him. Ashton smirked at me.

"Hermon is getting married," he replied.

I was blinking my eyes. Aleena would be devastated when she heard about *this*.

"Oh? And who's the lucky woman?" I asked. Again, Ashton smirked.

"Who said it was a woman? You know *his* sexual orientation, right?" Ashton asked. I nodded.

"I know, but don't you think his parents will—"

"I don't know if Hermon was telling the whole truth. He said that he would be gone for some time, and I didn't ask who the lucky person to be his partner was. He said that it was arranged between his family and them," Ashton said as I was nodding.

"I wish Aleena would not be so heartbroken when she finds out," I said before I was leaning against Ashton. He kissed my hair.

"Aleena also went out of the service. She said that she had something else to take care of. And Megan did not think much about it. She was rather...*preoccupied* at the moment," Ashton said as I was arching my eyebrow. He laughed.

"All will be revealed later, *liebling*. I know it will," Ashton said before he pulled me down beneath him as he was kissing me.

I know he was trying to distract me, but the question remains: Will Aleena find her happy ending? Was it with Hermon?

And what was keeping Megan so preoccupied that she did not bother when Aleena asked to resign?

Question upon the question, and I don't have the answers to them.

Don't miss out!

Visit the website below and you can sign up to receive emails whenever Nikki Larousse publishes a new book. There's no charge and no obligation.

https://books2read.com/r/B-A-QFQJB-YCWED

BOOKS2READ

Connecting independent readers to independent writers.

Did you love *Beneath the Mask*? Then you should read *The Croatian Crime*[1] by Nikki Larousse!

[2]

As an orphan, Mia Duncan suffered unimaginable atrocities at the hands of an organization that remained unreported until Detective Liam Hunt became involved in a case involving Mia Duncan. The group will do everything possible to keep Mia in its deception web.

Liam Hunt, driven by the killing of his parents, will stop at nothing to bring the culprit to justice. Only he had no idea that his parents' murderer was a lady who would later capture his affections and distort his judgment to do what was right.

---

1. https://books2read.com/u/baE9aa

2. https://books2read.com/u/baE9aa

Now they must work together to bring down the true bad people as well as the organization that ordered the murder of Liam's parents, and they must unearth a secret that might rip new holes in their already delicate relationship. Can Mia escape the fate planned for her, or will she forge her path with Liam by her side?

Also by Nikki Larousse

Bloodlines of the Nusantara
Blood and Fire of the Eternal Realm

Halloween Special Edition
The Irish Fire
The Evil Claim

Larouverse
The Croatian Crime
The French Fiasco
The Slavic Shamble
The Vlachs Vice
The Femme Fatale
The Italian Vow
The Spaniard Union
The American Marriage
The Albanian Promise
The Croesus' Brides

The Finnish Fiend
The Hungarian Hound

Niapachad Island
Dances of the Devious

Shifters of Cyprus
Shadow Pack
Kasun's Kisses
Beta's Bride
Gamma's Game
Delta's Deceit
Omega's Onslaught
Ultima's Upturn

STEAM Lovers
The Proposal Partner

The Dark Realm
Dark Discovery
Dark Seduction

About the Author

Nikki Larousse, who was reared in northeastern Malaysia, has always been enthralled with mythology from all around the world. She would always return to the escapism she found in writing things down, even if she had to focus on reality and pursue her higher education and work-life balance on the side. The majority of her creations are rooted in notorious Western myths, legends, and folklore. She does, however, also incorporate Malay folklore from her cultural background into her stories. So, if you dare to dream of cunning heroes and fierce heroines who battle together to achieve their happily ever-afters, enter her realms of Larouverse.

About the Publisher

In the quiet hours before dawn, when the world is asleep and only the hum of imagination stirs, **Nikki Larousse** writes. A storyteller at heart, she has always believed that words hold the power to shape worlds, evoke emotions, and leave an indelible mark on those who dare to dream. But beyond being an author, she envisioned something greater—a sanctuary for stories that defy convention, a home for narratives that refuse to be tamed.

Thus, **N.L. Ink Publishing** was born.

A Publisher Rooted in Passion

N.L. Ink Publishing isn't just a name; it's a testament to **independence, creative freedom, and the courage to write without boundaries.** As an **independent author and publisher,** Nikki Larousse carved out her own space in the literary world, unshackled by mainstream expectations. Her works thrive on complex characters, **morally grey dilemmas, and deeply immersive storytelling**, weaving together **romance, mystery, and the supernatural** in ways that linger long after the final page.

But N.L. Ink is more than a personal venture—it's a **beacon for authors who dream of publishing on their own terms.** In a world where traditional publishing often dictates what stories should be told, N.L. Ink stands as a reminder that **every voice deserves to be heard, every story deserves a chance.**

A Legacy in Ink

The *quill* in the publisher's logo is more than a symbol—it's a promise. A promise that *words matter, stories endure, and ink is eternal.* The **circular stroke** around it represents the *never-ending cycle of inspiration*, where one tale leads to another, sparking creativity across generations.

From the first draft to the final publication, Nikki Larousse understands the struggles, the doubts, and the triumphs of being an independent author. N.L. Ink Publishing is **not just a business—it's a mission**: to uplift, empower, and prove that great stories don't need permission to exist.

And so, with every book published under its name, *N.L. Ink continues to carve its legacy—one story, one word, one inked dream at a time.*